The Imaginary Garden

For my mom, who tends to her own imaginary garden.
With thanks to Yvette for helping me to tend mine — A.L.

For Mom and Dad, a.k.a. "Ya-Ya" and "Opa" — I.L.

Text © 2009 Andrew Larsen
Illustrations © 2009 Irene Luxbacher

Kids Can Press acknowledges the financial support of the Government of
Ontario, through the Ontario Media Development Corporation's Ontario Book
Initiative; the Ontario Arts Council; the Canada Council for the Arts; and the
Government of Canada, through the BPIDP, for our publishing activity.

Published in Canada by
Kids Can Press Ltd.
29 Birch Avenue
Toronto, ON M4V 1E2

Published in the U.S. by
Kids Can Press Ltd.
2250 Military Road
Tonawanda, NY 14150

www.kidscanpress.com

The artwork in this book was rendered in pen and ink and multimedia collage.
The text is set in Goudy.

Edited by Yvette Ghione
Designed by Marie Bartholomew
Printed and bound in China

This book is smyth sewn casebound.

CM 09 0 9 8 7 6 5 4 3 2 1

Library and Archives Canada Cataloguing in Publication
Larsen, Andrew, 1960–
      The imaginary garden / written by Andrew Larsen ; illustrated
by Irene Luxbacher.

Interest age level: For ages 3–7.
ISBN 978-1-55453-279-7

I. Luxbacher, Irene, 1970– II. Title.

PS8623.A77I53 2009   jC813'.6   C2008-903323-X

Kids Can Press is a Corus™ Entertainment company

The Imaginary Garden

Andrew Larsen ♥ Irene Luxbacher

Kids Can Press

Theo loved Poppa's old house.
She loved Poppa's old garden.
Poppa used to tell Theo all about the different flowers while they sat together under the maple tree.

Poppa's new apartment didn't have a garden.

"Are you going to put flowers out here on the balcony?" asked Theo one day.

"I think it's too windy for flowers," answered Poppa.

"What about plastic flowers?" suggested Theo. "We can fill the whole balcony."

"Hmmm," said Poppa. "Then it would be a plastic garden."

"I know!" said Theo. "We could have an imaginary garden."

Poppa's eyes lit up.

Theo and Poppa planned their imaginary
garden before spring had even come.

On the first Saturday of spring, Poppa bought a great big blank canvas. He also bought a pair of matching gardening hats for himself and Theo. Poppa put the canvas out on the balcony.

Theo looked at the canvas. "What should we do first?" she asked.

"Let's put a stone wall at the back of the garden," answered Poppa. "The vines will need to hold onto something as they reach for the sun."

Poppa got out his paints. He mixed a bit of white
and a bit of black. Together they made gray.

Stroke by stroke, stone by stone, Poppa built a wall.
It stretched from one side of the garden to the other.
Above the stone wall, Theo painted a soft blue sky.

Then Poppa mixed some green, some red and some blue. Together they made brown. He spread the paint at the foot of the wall, creating a bed of soil.

"There! But that's enough work for one day," Poppa
said. "Next time we'll be ready to do some planting."
"Poppa, I love gardening with you," said Theo.
"And I love gardening with you, Theo," said Poppa.

On Monday afternoon, Poppa and Theo went
back into the garden.
"The garden is waking up after a long winter,"
said Poppa as he dipped his brush into the green paint.
He painted tiny stems.
"The first flowers coming up are crocuses,"
he continued. "And look at all the scilla!"

Poppa dotted the crocus stems with little drops
of color: Yellow. Purple. White.

Theo dotted the scilla stems with little drops of color: Blue. Blue. Blue.

"What now, Poppa?" asked Theo.
Poppa put a dab of red just above
the stone wall.

And there was a wing.

He added a small dab of brown.
There was a head.
Then he swept around the red with
brushes of brown.

Next he made three neat yellow jots.
There was a beak. And there was a pair
of skinny legs.
Then he added a single black dot.
There was an eye.

There was a tail.

"It must be spring! A robin has come to visit our garden," said Poppa.

"Look! He's having lunch," added Theo. She painted a tiny pink earthworm in the robin's beak.

"He's not the only one who is hungry," laughed Poppa. "Let's get ourselves a snack, too."

A few weeks later, Poppa prepared to
leave on holiday. He asked Theo to take care of the garden.

"But, Poppa, how will I know what to do?" Theo worried.
She had never gardened by herself before.

"Well, the tulips and daffodils should blossom while I'm
away," said Poppa. "And the vines should begin to climb the
wall." He kissed her on each cheek. "Don't fret, Theodora.
When you see the garden, you'll know just what to do."

On Sunday morning, Theo looked into the garden.
The crocuses and scilla were gone. The garden was filled
with a new growth of stems. And the vines had begun their
climb up the stone wall, just like Poppa said they would.

Theo put on her gardening hat and picked up
a paintbrush. She knew just what to do.

She topped the tulip stems with blooms of color:
Orange. Purple. Pink.

She topped the daffodil stems with blooms of
color: Yellow. Yellow. Yellow.

But something was missing ...

Then Theo remembered: Blue. Blue. Blue.
Forget-me-nots, Poppa's favorite flower.

But still there was something missing.
Theo thought and thought.

Then, smiling, she added
a few dashes to the back of
the garden against the gray
stone wall.
"There!" she said.

Theo could hardly wait until Poppa returned from his holiday.

By Poppa and Theo